P9-DEE-614

Library of Congress Cataloging-in-Publication Data

Holland, Isabelle.
The Christmas cat.
Summary: A homeless cat, dog, and donkey follow a star to see a king and find their lives changing as a result.
[1. Jesus Christ—Nativity—Fiction. 2. Christmas—Fiction. 3. Animals—Fiction] I. Mitchell, Kathy, ill. II. Title.
PZ7.H7083Ch 1987 [E] 86-23409
ISBN: 0-307-16542-6
ISBN: 0-307-66542-9 (lib. bdg.)

THE CHRISTMAS CAT

By Isabelle Holland
Illustrated by Kathy Mitchell

A GOLDEN BOOK • NEW YORK
Western Publishing Company, Inc., Racine, Wisconsin 53404

 B C D E F G H I J K L M

Peter was a stray who lived on the street. He had no mother or father or family, and he was always hungry. Nobody would feed him. So he ate scraps that people threw away. But when they saw him, people often yelled, "Scat!" and flung things at him. Then he would have to try another street.

"He's just a stray," he heard somebody say. "He's not important."

"I'm not important," Peter thought sadly. "But who *is* important?"

One night Peter looked through the window of a rich house and saw a dog with a jeweled collar sitting on a silken cushion.

"Who are you?" he asked, gazing hungrily at the dog's dish full of delicious food.

"I'm important," the proud dog said.

"If you're not going to eat, may I please have some of your food?" Peter asked timidly. His stomach was empty.

"Certainly not!" the dog snarled. "Go away, you beggar!" And he barked and lunged at Peter.

Peter ran.

It was dark and cold. Peter had not eaten anything since the day before. He decided to try another street.

He went around a corner and found himself in a big square. There were lights in the doorways of the buildings, and people were standing around talking. Everybody seemed excited about something. In the middle of the square were more people and soldiers with camels and donkeys loaded with sacks.

"I wonder if food is in those sacks," Peter thought. But the animals were too high and the sacks too firmly tied for Peter to find out.

Tired and discouraged, he slunk around the edges of the square, sniffing at open doors to see if there were any scraps of food. But every time he found something, somebody would yell, "You, cat—out!" and a stone or a piece of wood would come sailing past his head. Finally he lay down. He was too weary and too hungry even to try anymore.

He was sitting by a corner of a building when he heard another voice yelling. This voice said, "You, dog—out!" A door opened, and a stone came hurtling past Peter's head. Right afterward, a thin dog with his tail between his legs came running past. But another stone hit the dog, and he fell near Peter.

When the door had slammed, Peter crawled near the dog. Blood was coming from a cut on his head. "What's your name?" he asked. "Mine's Peter."

The dog said wearily, "Once, a long time ago, it was Caleb. But I can't remember who gave it to me. Now everybody just calls me 'You, dog—out!'"

They sat there together. Both were very tired and hungry. After a while, Peter started licking Caleb's cut and it stopped bleeding. The night was getting cold, but huddled together they were warmer.

"If only somebody would throw out some food," Peter thought.

Just then the door behind them opened and somebody emptied a bag into the street. Then the door closed.

Almost afraid to believe it might be food, Peter raised his head and sniffed. Then he got up and ran to the doorway. "Caleb, come quickly," he called. "It's meat."

There wasn't a lot, but there was enough for both to make a meal. Afterward, they found an even better corner, away from the light, and they went to sleep.

Noise woke Peter, and he peered around the edge of their hiding place. The camels and donkeys were beginning to form a procession to leave the square by the big gate opposite.

"Where are they going?" somebody asked a few feet away.

Another person answered, "Nobody knows. The leaders of the caravan say they're following something. But the others don't seem to know what it is."

"Where do they come from?"

The first man shrugged. "From the East somewhere. People say they're taking presents to a king."

Caleb was awake now. "What's a present?" he asked Peter.

"I don't know," Peter said. Far back in his memory something stirred—something his mother had said, something about a king. But he couldn't quite remember it.

They watched for a few minutes as the animals paraded out of the square. "I bet all those people and animals have food with them," Caleb said. "Maybe we ought to follow them."

"But if they chased us away," Peter said, "then we might be in the middle of nowhere with nothing to eat." Peter had never left the city. "Have you ever been outside the walls?" he asked Caleb.

"Once, when some men chased me out."

"What was it like?"

"Dark—and when the sun went down, cold. I lay next to the wall all night and listened to a mountain lion growling not too far away. When it was dawn and the gate was opened, I ran back in."

Peter looked at him. "I think you're brave, wanting to go out there again. Of course, we won't be alone. Even if they chase us, we can stay near the caravan." He stared at the bulging sacks on the donkeys and camels. "Do you think they're all full of food?"

"Sure to be," Caleb replied. He hesitated. "Maybe some are carrying those presents the men talked about—whatever presents are."

"Oh," Peter began, "those things they're taking to the king."

Peter could almost hear his mother's voice now as she talked to him when he was a kitten, and licked him, and told him wise things, and said something about a king. Suddenly he was quite sure she would want them to follow the caravan, to go with the people who were going to see a king.

"I think we ought to go," he said, and they dashed across the big square.

As they followed the caravan out of the city and toward the mountain pass, his mother's words sprang into his mind. "Remember, Peter," she had said, "a cat may look at a king."

He repeated it over to himself twice. The words made him feel warm and full of hope.

"A cat may look at a king," he said to Caleb.

"We'd never be allowed to look at a king," Caleb said. "We're not important."

The first night the caravan rested, Peter and Caleb hid in a cave and watched as the people threw out scraps of food when they had finished eating. Then they waited until the people were all asleep and came out of the cave to feast on what they could find.

They were about to creep back to their hiding place when they heard the sound of someone crying. They both stopped. Then they crept toward one of the tents. There, tied to a stake outside the tent, was a very small donkey. His back was covered with cuts and stripes.

"What's the matter?" whispered Peter and Caleb.

"My mother died just before we left," the donkey said. "And they are trying to make me carry her load, too. When I fall, they whip me."

"You'd better come with us," Peter said. "We stay behind the caravan and hide in caves and eat the scraps they throw out. Nobody sees us and we have plenty to eat."

"They will kill you if they see you," the donkey whispered. "They don't allow cats and dogs near the camp. People are cruel. I saw one of the servants beat a dog to death."

"We know people are cruel," Caleb said. "Peter and I don't have homes, and nobody would give us anything to eat—not even the food they were throwing out."

"All people aren't cruel," Peter said.

"Have you ever known a people who was kind to you?" Caleb asked.

Peter thought for a moment. An old memory stirred in his mind, a memory of warmth and good food, of a soft voice and a gentle hand stroking him.

"Yes," Peter said. The memory made him both happy and sad. "It was a people with a kind voice and a gentle hand."

"My mother had a wonderful voice," the donkey said. "And she'd rub me with her face."

"But she wasn't a people," Caleb said. "She was a donkey." He turned to Peter. "I bet it was your mother you were thinking about. And she wasn't a people. She was an animal. Animals are fine. It's people who are bad."

"I don't know," Peter said. "I still think it was a people, but you may be right. Anyway," he said to the donkey, "you'd better come with us."

"I'm tied. How can I get free?"

"I got beaten once for chewing a cord when I was a puppy," Caleb said. "Let me try."

Both Caleb and Peter chewed and chewed and chewed. After what seemed like a long time, the donkey pulled on the rope and was able to break it.

"Now," Peter said, "let's go back into the caves. What's your name?"

"Balaam," the donkey said. "After the man who owned one of my ancestors."

The next morning they left their cave and followed the caravan as it approached the top of the mountain pass. "Are you sure it's a good idea to follow them?" Balaam asked anxiously.

"Yes. They throw away food," Caleb said.

"And we'll get to see the king," Peter added.

"What makes you think the king will see us?" Balaam asked. "Kings see only people who are important."

"My mother said a cat may look at a king, and I'm sure she was right."

"But we're not cats," Caleb and Balaam said together.

"I'm a cat, and you're my friends."

They traveled for many days and nights. They kept far enough back so the people in the caravan could not see them, but not so far that the bandits and wild animals in the mountains would attack them. Finally one night the caravan left the high mountains and came down into the desert. It was then—when Peter and Caleb and Balaam left the pass, and there were no more peaks or jutting rocks to hide the sky—that they saw it.

"Look!" Balaam whispered, staring up at the great shining star in front of the caravan.

"I've never seen anything so bright," Caleb said.

"Or so large," Balaam said, a little nervously.

"It's like a huge light," Peter said.

They stared at it for a while.

"What do you think it means?" Caleb asked.

"Something dangerous?" Balaam whispered.

Peter suddenly found himself thinking about his old memory of the warmth, the tender voice, and the gentle hand. "No," he said. "I think it's something good."

It seemed to get bigger and brighter as they talked. The sky behind it was like black velvet. In front of them, the caravan had stopped. All the men and soldiers were standing, staring at the brilliant star. Everything and everyone was still.

And then Balaam sneezed.

"Who is that?" the men who were nearest yelled. And they came striding toward where Peter and Caleb and Balaam cowered.

"Run!" Peter said.

They ran as fast as they could, trying to take cover behind bushes and rocks when the men seemed near enough to pounce on them.

"It's those pests from the city," one man said as Peter slid past his outstretched hand. "I'll get them yet."

"That's my master's donkey," another cried. "Come here, you!" The man grabbed a rope and took off after Balaam.

Their hearts pounding, Peter and Caleb and Balaam ran as fast as they could. But there were no caves to hide in and they knew that soon, when they couldn't run anymore, they would be caught.

The men, laughing and jeering, with ropes and knives in their hands, were gaining on them.

And then a very strange thing happened. A cloud passed in front of the great star. The huge light was covered. The desert was dark once more.

"Where are those pests?" one of the men said. "I can't see a thing."

Peter and Caleb and Balaam, cowering in the sand behind a small bush, barely allowed themselves to breathe. They could feel the men almost on top of them, and they were afraid to move.

"Oh, let them go," a second man said. "If we linger here, we might lose sight of the caravan, and we'd never find it again here in the desert. I hadn't realized we'd run so far. Look, the camp fires seem far away."

"We'd better get back quickly," a third man said. "Dawn will be here soon, and they might leave without us."

Peter and Caleb and Balaam lay behind the bush, huddled together for warmth and courage, listening to the men's voices getting fainter as they returned to the caravan. Finally there was silence.

"What are we going to do now?" Balaam whispered. "We are out in the desert with no food, and they will kill us if they find us."

"I *told* you all people are wicked," Caleb said.

"I'll think of something," Peter said.

"Why don't we go back to the city?" Caleb suggested. "We'll be hungry till we arrive, but at least we won't be chased by those men."

Peter didn't speak for a moment, mostly because he couldn't think of anything helpful to say. Finally he said, "Let's take a nap. We're going to need our rest."

"Maybe *you* can sleep," Balaam said, sounding aggrieved.

But they all slept.

Peter dreamed about his mother. Quite clearly he heard her voice say, "Remember, Peter, a cat may look at a king."

Then he woke up. It was dawn. A huge orange sun was coming up over the edge of the desert. The caravan was just disappearing over the horizon.

"Wake up, Caleb! Wake up, Balaam! We have to catch up with the caravan!"

"Why?" Caleb and Balaam asked together. "Aren't we going back to the city?"

"No," Peter said. "We're going to see the king."

"Won't they come after us?" Balaam asked anxiously.

"I've told you," Caleb said to Peter, "the king doesn't want to see us. We're not important."

"And besides," Balaam put in, "he's a people. And you know what *they're* like."

"Well, I'm going," Peter said. "Mother said a cat may look at a king, and she was always right."

Caleb and Balaam sighed. "All right," Caleb said.

"If you insist," Balaam added.

They plodded on, going from bush to bush and from rock to rock so the people far in the front with the caravan wouldn't be able to see them.

That night Peter said, "I wonder if that great star is the thing that the caravan is following, the way those people back at the square said."

"Whatever it is, it's not for us," Balaam said.

"I guess not," Caleb agreed.

"Why not?" Peter said. "After all, we see the light, too." He felt he had to keep everyone's spirits up. He knew it was on his account that they were in the middle of the desert, following a caravan filled with people who would kill them if they could.

The days and nights wore on. People in the caravan still threw out scraps that Peter, Caleb, and Balaam ate when they were sure no one was looking. But as time passed, the food got less.

"What I'd like," Caleb said wistfully, "is a bone to chew."

"What I'd like," Balaam said, "is a wisp of hay and some oats."

"What I'd like," Peter said, "is to see the king, and after that, a nice piece of meat."

Sometimes when they crept up to the tents, they would hear men discussing where the king might live. None of them knew where it would be, but they all agreed that he would live in a great city, in a palace with soldiers and guards and courtiers and many servants.

So when the big star suddenly stopped in front of them and the caravan came to a halt, they were quite sure that they had reached a city and would find the king's palace inside the walls. There was a great bustle as all the men talked excitedly among themselves.

"How many followers are our kings taking with them?" one man asked.

"They will need some of us to carry their gifts," another said.

"What are they presenting to this king?" a third asked. "No one was able to tell me."

"They say the gifts are of gold, frankincense, and myrrh."

"Gold for a king, frankincense for a priest..." the first man said.

"And myrrh for the tomb," the third man answered.

Everyone was quiet for a moment.

"You didn't tell me there were kings in the caravan," Caleb said to Peter.

"I didn't know. But let's go up and look at them." He was still thinking about what his mother had told him.

"They'll eat us for dinner," Balaam said.

"Well, I'm going," Peter said, sounding much braver than he felt.

Keeping far to the side of the caravan, they crept forward, darting quickly from bush to rock. Luckily everyone was too excited over having arrived to pay them any attention. When they finally reached the front of the caravan, they stopped in astonishment. There was no great walled city in front of them. Only a few houses were scattered beyond and around. Directly in front, built into a sort of cave in the side of a rocky hill, was a stable.

In the stable, nestled in the straw, was a young woman, and on her lap was a baby wrapped in cloth. Behind them stood a young man, looking down at both of them, and around, also looking at them, were a cow, a donkey, a few sheep, and a dog. Beside the animals kneeled some roughly clothed shepherds. As they gazed at the baby their faces shone with happiness.

Behind the shepherds, at the edge of the stable, were three tall men, richly dressed, bearing in their hands the gifts they had brought for the king. There was total silence. The huge star, now right above the stable, poured its light over them all.

Without even thinking, or worrying about being caught, Peter, Caleb, and Balaam found themselves creeping farther and farther forward until they were right behind the three kings.

They watched as the men took their presents up and held them before the baby.

"He's a people," Balaam said wonderingly, looking at the baby, "but even so, he's wonderful."

"He would never chase us," Caleb said.

"Or beat us," Peter said.

"Or let us go hungry," Balaam said.

And without thinking, all three walked forward into the stable, sat down among the other animals, and gazed at the baby.

After a while, Peter said to Caleb and Balaam, "I think the baby is looking at us."

"Yes," Caleb said. "I think so, too."

Balaam nodded. "Yes," he said. "Oh, yes."

Soon Peter was filled with a sensation that he had never felt before and that he had no name for.

"I'm feeling something very strange," he said to the other two.

"Me, too," Caleb and Balaam said together.

"I think," Peter said, "I think it's called happy."

"It's wonderful," Balaam whispered. He turned his head a little and gave a gasp. "Caleb," he said, "I never realized how handsome you are! You're the handsomest dog I've ever seen."

Instead of looking scrawny and half-starved, with a dirty coat and a skinny tail, Caleb had a thick, shiny russet coat, and his tail had wavy plumes of the same color.

"You, too," Caleb said. "And Peter."

Balaam's coat was now glossy. All his wounds and cuts had healed. And Peter! Peter's fur was a shimmering black, and his eyes shone with green fire.

The great star poured its light down on them.

Then there was a sudden uproar as some of the men from the caravan rushed up. "Those are the pests we thought we'd chased away," one of the soldiers said. "Somebody must have fed them. I almost didn't recognize them. We'll take them back and get rid of them." He glanced at the baby. "Is that the king?"

"The King of Kings," one of the three kings said. "And what animals are you talking about?"

"Those!" The soldier started after Peter, Caleb, and Balaam. They began to back away, but there was nowhere they could go.

"Oh, King of Kings, help us!" Peter whispered.

"But they're beautiful," one of the three kings said.

"That is a small, very pretty donkey," another king said to the soldier. "Leave him be. I shall take him home to my son as a present."

"And I shall take that fine dog," the second king said. "He shall be a present for my daughter."

"I think I'll take that handsome cat," the third king said. "I like the way he's looking at me. Come here, all of you!"

Peter, Caleb, and Balaam came forward, not believing what they had heard. The kings patted and stroked them. Peter, remembering the gentle hand of long ago, purred. He had forgotten that he had that deep rumble inside himself.

"Soldier!" one of the kings called. The soldier stepped forward. "Take these three fine gifts for our families, and give them something to eat and a warm place to sleep. They're important," the king said.

"Did you hear that?" Peter said. "We're important."

The soldier led them to a big tent and bowed low as he held the flap for them. "Food will be brought," the soldier said. "Take your ease."

The floor of the tent was covered with a thick carpet, and there were soft cushions all around.

Peter and Caleb and Balaam had barely sat down before a servant came in with dishes full of meat for Peter and Caleb, oats and hay for Balaam, and a large bowl of water.

They ate every bite and drank deeply of the clear water.

"I can barely believe this is happening," Balaam said.

Caleb settled himself among the cushions. "And these are PEOPLE being good to us."

"I told you people could be good," Peter said. A great rumbling purr of happiness was beginning deep in his middle. "I'll never forget the way the star shone," he said.

"Or the way the King of Kings looked at us." Balaam twitched his ears. "I know he was only a baby. But you could tell he was the King of Kings."

"I'm glad we were together," Peter said. "I hope we'll be together where we're going."

"Yes," the other two said.

Caleb added, "I heard one of the soldiers say something about everybody coming from the same place, so I'm sure we will be."

Peter stretched, admiring the new shine on his fur. "You see? My mother was right—a cat may look at a king."